Doodlebug

A Novel in Doodles

by

Karen Romano Young

SQUARE
FISH

FEIWEL AND FRIENDS
NEW YORK

SQUARE FISH

An Imprint of Macmillan

Square Fish and the Square Fish logo are trademarks of Macmillan and
are used by Feiwel and Friends under license from Macmillan.

Library of Congress Cataloging-in-Publication Data Available
ISBN 978-1-250-01020-9

Originally published in the United States by Feiwel and Friends
First Square Fish Edition: October 2012
Square Fish logo designed by Filomena Tuosto
Book designed by Kathleen Breitenfeld
mackids.com

10 9 8 7 6 5 4 3 2 1

AR: 3.3 / LEXILE: 520L

For Emily, with love from Schmuel.

Thank you, KATIE DAVIS !!!

Thank you, J. Alison James and
the MARCH MADNESS authors.

Thank you, Bill, Staci, and SVEN.

Thank you, NOON, for the buck teeth.

(The End.)

☐1. L.A.

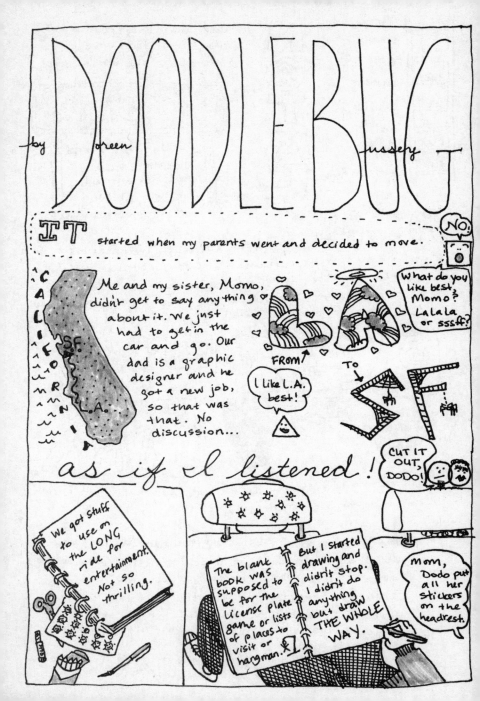

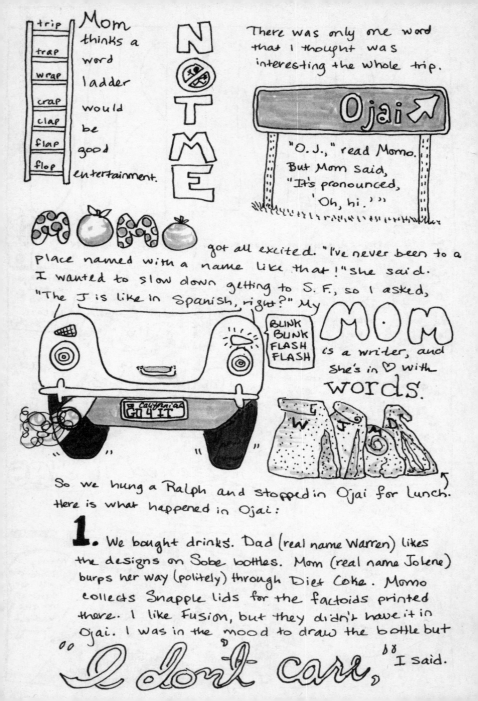

trip / trap / wrap / crap / clap / flap / flop

Mom thinks a word ladder would be good entertainment.

NOT ME

There was only one word that I thought was interesting the whole trip.

Ojai ↗

"O.J.," read Momo. But Mom said, "It's pronounced, 'Oh, hi.'"

MoMo got all excited. "I've never been to a place named with a name like that!" she said. I wanted to slow down getting to S.F., so I asked, "The J is like in Spanish, right?" My MOM is a writer, and she's in ♡ with words.

BLINK BUNK FLASH FLASH

California GO 4 IT

So we hung a Ralph and stopped in Ojai for lunch. Here is what happened in Ojai:

1. We bought drinks. Dad (real name Warren) likes the designs on Sobe bottles. Mom (real name Jolene) burps her way (politely) through Diet Coke. Momo collects Snapple lids for the factoids printed there. I like Fusion, but they didn't have it in Ojai. I was in the mood to draw the bottle but "I don't care," I said.

2. I didn't want to talk. So I got my blank book out of the car and tried drawing this cool tower.

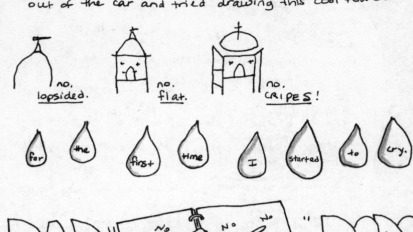

no, <u>lopsided.</u>

no, <u>flat.</u>

no, CRIPES!

for the first time I started to cry.

DAD came over and looked at my paper. I yelled like a freak.

DON'T LOOK! No No No No No No No No

"DODO," he said. "Just keep drawing."

Here, Dad.

I finally finished. →

They had let us stay in Ojai until I got the picture of the post office tower to look more or less O.K.

"I didn't think you were ever going to stop drawing," said

Momo. I said, "Maybe I won't stop!"

Oh hi, Ojai!

ZZZZZzzz...

Momo started snoring right away.

"How about you?" Mom asked me.

"Are you going to faire dodo?"

♪♪♪fais dodo♪♪♪ is a song.

I'm not sleeping, hahaha.

I'm not French, either!

My mom loves words in any language.

She used to sing to me,

"fais dodo, ma petite cherie."

It means "make sleep, my little dear." (Not cherry!)

BUT I NEVER DID.

Hahaha. My name is Doreen. But Dodo stuck.

Momo's name means "peach" in Japanese.

We're not Japanese, either.

Mom found the name in a book called Umbrella.
The little girl in Umbrella is named Momo.

I said, Why didn't you name her Umbrella ?

Because my mom just likes words, get it?
(Momo's real name is Maureen.)

Warren (39) (DAD) Jolene (MOM) (41)

Doreen (12) (DODO) Maureen (MOMO) (10½)

= 4 All the people I know in all San Francisco.

age total: 102½

We drove another hundred miles, and Momo made ZZZZs. I drew some more. I was having a lot of **DARK** thoughts about what was at the other end of this road.

RATS!!!!!!

"Are we going to stop anywhere else?" I asked.

"How about that almond stand?" said Dad.

The ☀ was warm like the stickers on the headrest, and Momo stayed asleep as we bought almonds.

"You know, Dodo," said Mom. "In a new school you can be a whole new person. You can be ANYONE YOU WANT."

NUTS!!!!!

I liked my old school.
I knew who everybody was.
I knew where everything was.
I didn't have to be a whole new person.
I could be myself.
I want to go HOME.

"Fine then!!!"

I said.

"From now on, my name is...

→

Doodlebug

Mom was driving, so I handed my book to Dad.

"Doodlebug," he read. He showed the page to Mom. "ART IS POWER," he said.

Mom said, "THE PEN IS MIGHTIER THAN THE SWORD." Then she said, "Shut up please, everyone. This road is getting very curly."

Dad gave me back my book. He said, "ROCK ON, DODO." I said, "Doodlebug!" And I added, "I rule!" "You DROOL," said momo

FACT #1: making all those dots, I felt the POWER

FACT #2: Mom did say curly, not curvy.

AND IT WAS GETTING cliffy.

"Do you want me to drive?" asked Dad sweetly.

"NO!" said Mom unsweetly.

"You don't have to be such a hero," said Dad.

BUT even after we stopped at a fruit stand, she drove.

"We've got to face our fears, MOM." said

Momo ate a peach. I drew strawberries. Dad worried.

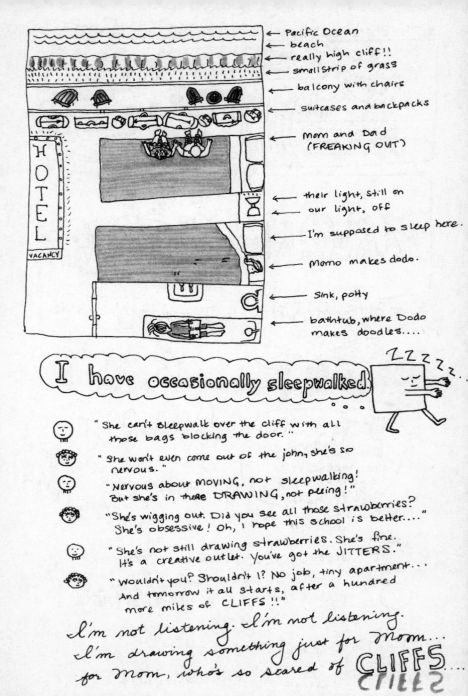

* white knuckles

Mom survived.

"Did my funeral help?"

"What is your PROBLEM?" asked Momo.

"It was the WORST-CASE SCENARIO," said Dad.

"And that means what?"

What's the worst that could HAPPEN? (said Dad.)   24 miles

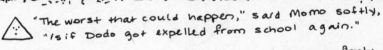

"The worst that could happen," said Momo softly, "is if Dodo got expelled from school again."

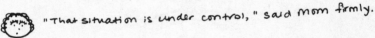

"That situation is under control," said Mom firmly.

"It wasn't your fault anyway," murmured Dad.

"YES, IT WAS!" I exclaimed. "IT WAS <u>ONLY MY FAULT</u>!"

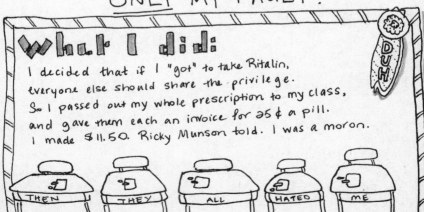

what I did:

I decided that if I "got" to take Ritalin, everyone else should share the privilege. So I passed out my whole prescription to my class, and gave them each an invoice for 25¢ a pill. I made $11.50. Ricky Munson told. I was a moron.

DUH

THEN   THEY   ALL   HATED   ME

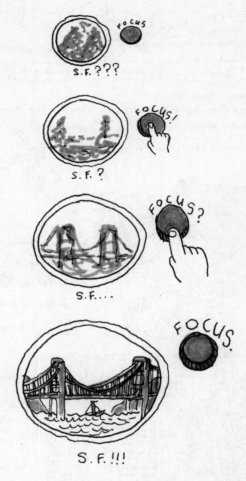

FOCUS

S.F.???

FOCUS!

S.F.?

FOCUS?

S.F....

FOCUS.

S.F.!!!

(Getting There.)

2. S.F.

THE OCEAN LOOKS DIFFERENT NEAR SAN FRANCISCO

Everything Happens at the Right Time

Mom has sayings.
She says this one now, brightly. (Shut up Shut up Shut up!)

😐 | Dodo | did | what | she | thought | she | needed | to | do.

Dad makes statements.
Sometimes I wonder if he mixes up his words like magnetic poems.

(Shut shut shut up up up!)

Then he added, "When you see a 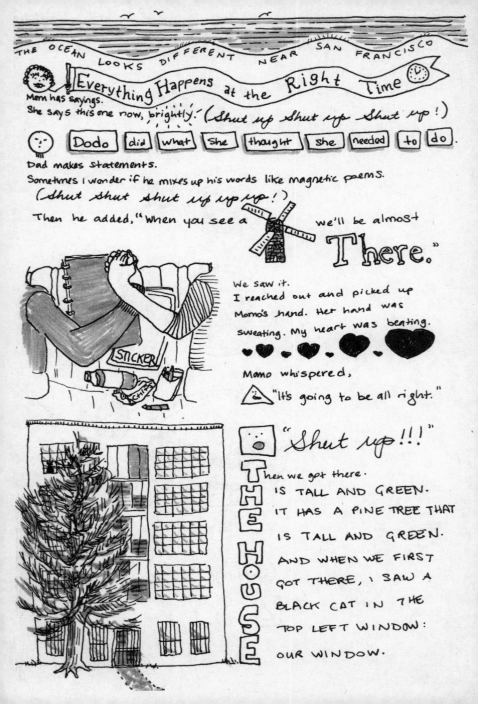 we'll be almost **There.**"

We saw it.
I reached out and picked up
Momo's hand. Her hand was
sweating. My heart was beating.

♥ ♥ ♥ • ♥ ♥ ♥

Momo whispered,

△ "It's going to be all right."

😮 **"Shut up!!!"**

THE HOUSE

Then we got there.
IS TALL AND GREEN.
IT HAS A PINE TREE THAT
IS TALL AND GREEN.
AND WHEN WE FIRST
GOT THERE, I SAW A
BLACK CAT IN THE
TOP LEFT WINDOW:
OUR WINDOW.

STICKER

3 months!

JANUARY FEBRUARY MARCH

That is how long we have in this apartment.

It is a sublet. It's Staci's apartment. Staci is Dad's college friend who is in Japan. The only thing I knew about Staci before now is a picture she made in illustration class for an assignment. They had to illustrate an everyday saying. Staci did "buck teeth" and it looked like this:

They are antlers growing out of crooked teeth.

Dad had hung it on his office wall in L.A. Where was it now?

He says it was the beginning of Staci's dental art. Momo, who has braces, thought he meant those colored thingers you can get on your braces for your color-coordinated outfit. But Dad picked up a DVD and said, "This is her." Staci is an animator now. She made:

Mouth the Almighty

Mouth the **A**lmighty was a superhero set of choppers with feet, arms, eyes, and a gum-pink cape. On the back of the DVD it said,

Her bite is worse than her bark.

"Ouch," said Dad. "That's Staci for ya."

STACI'S	LIVING ROOM	WINDOW	LOOKED OUT	INTO THE	BIG TREE.
MOMO	AND I WERE	GOING TO	SLEEP ON THE	DAYBED HERE	THAT
HAD A	QUILT WITH	THE PATTERN	OF "FLYING	GEESE." I	KNOW
FROM A	REPORT I DID:	SLAVES HUNG	THIS QUILT	WHEN IT WAS	TIME
TO RUN	AWAY.	UNDER THE	BED WE	FOUND SVEN.	HISS!!

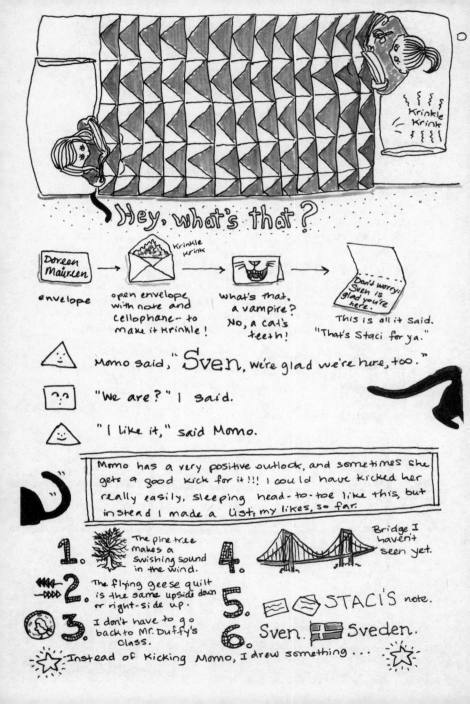

Krinkle Krink

Hey, what's that?

Doreen Maureen — envelope → open envelope with note and cellophane- to make it krinkle! → Krinkle Krink — what's that, a vampire? No, a cat's teeth! → Don't worry: Sven is glad you're here. This is all it said. "That's Staci for ya."

Momo said, "Sven, we're glad we're here, too."

"We are?" I said.

"I like it," said Momo.

Momo has a very positive outlook, and sometimes she gets a good kick for it!!! I could have kicked her really easily, sleeping head-to-toe like this, but instead I made a list, my likes, so far.

1. The pine tree makes a swishing sound in the wind.

2. The flying geese quilt is the same upside down or right-side up.

3. I don't have to go back to Mr. Duffy's class.

4. Bridge I haven't seen yet.

5. STACI'S note.

6. Sven. Sveden.

Instead of kicking Momo, I drew something . . .

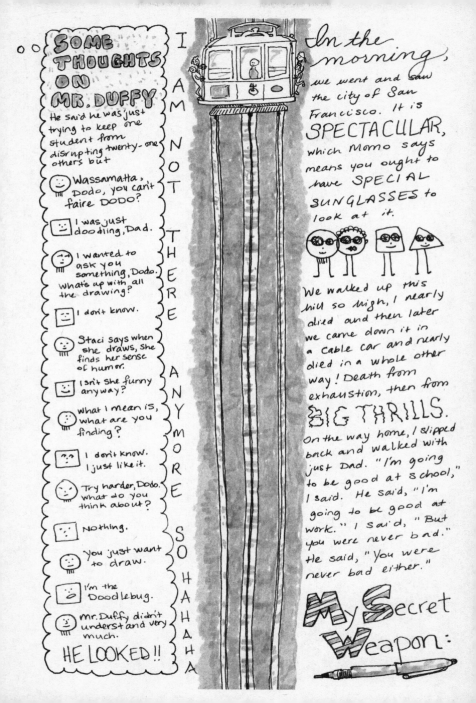

SOME THOUGHTS ON MR. DUFFY

He said he was just trying to keep one student from disrupting twenty-one others but

— Wassamatta, Dodo, you can't faire DODO?

— I was just doodling, Dad.

— I wanted to ask you something, Dodo. What's up with all the drawing?

— I don't know.

— Staci says when she draws, she finds her sense of humor.

— Isn't she funny anyway?

— What I mean is, what are you finding?

— I don't know. I just like it.

— Try harder, Dodo. What do you think about?

— Nothing.

— You just want to draw.

— I'm the Doodlebug.

— Mr. Duffy didn't understand very much.

HE LOOKED!!

I AM NOT THERE ANYMORE SO HAHAHA

In the morning, we went and saw the city of San Francisco. It is SPECTACULAR, which Momo says means you ought to have SPECIAL SUNGLASSES to look at it.

We walked up this hill so high, I nearly died and then later we came down it in a cable car and nearly died in a whole other way! Death from exhaustion, then from BIG THRILLS.

On the way home, I slipped back and walked with just Dad. "I'm going to be good at school," I said. He said, "I'm going to be good at work." I said, "But you were never bad." He said, "You were never bad either."

My Secret Weapon:

3. STUPID OLD NEW SCHOOL STARTS

visibles:

~~invisables:~~ *
invisibles: *

Sweater
(It's cold here.)

oh, you know.

Skirt
(I'm trying to
make a good
impression.)

what would really
be embarrassing
would be NOT
wearing them.

bally socks

penny for luck

Vanny vans

Band·Aid in
case of unluck
(blister)

* so secret, I forgot how to spell it,
but just for a second

SUNDAY

I...DON'T...LIKE...SUNDAY...BECAUSE...TOMORROW...IS......

Monday.

THIS IS OUR SCHOOL →

MIDDLE SCHOOL

MOMO THINKS IT'S COOL →

It has columns but they are not Doric columns, which might be a good omen!

It looks like a wedding cake or a mission or a museum or a library!

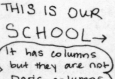

They're Corinthian columns, all carved and pretty.

Don't the trees remind you of Mom's curly hair?

7th grade

5th grade

Our old school was a little private school.

This school is a big public school. Eek!

A Venn diagram:

Dad's opinions:

"You won't be just stuck in one classroom!"

"You might hear some more swearing."

"Junior high is cruelty on a cracker."

Shared opinions:

You'll be able to move around more.

You won't be the only loon in the lake.

Good luck. You'll need it!

Mom's opinions:

"You'll have a different teacher for every class!"

"You'll be with a more diverse group."

"They oughta build a moat around 7th grade."

Have some cheese with that.

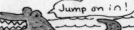

Jump on in!

FIRST DAY PRECAUTIONS:

 Take $ for lunch until you figure out what people do.

Touch Sven's tail for good luck.
(He's still under the bed, dreaming of Sweden.)

 Take Doodlebook to help you remember who you are.

 Take turned-off cellphone. Get told to give it to Momo to hold just in case you're going to get nervous and use bad judgment and call someone. Take it back from Momo the second you're inside the school door.

WOMEN Notice where the loo-loo is just in case you have to barf, which seems likely. (In our old school, it said GIRLS.)

 Study the EMERGENCY Building Exit sign. This is always a good idea, even better when you're scared to look at all the other MIDDLE SCHOOL STUDENTS entering. (Basically, the sign says if something catches up or blows fire * turn around and leave the building. DUH.)

 (((SO I'M A LITTLE NERVOUS. SUE ME!))) *

* Yes, I wrote it inside out. I like it that way!

my Vans were plain white but I made them plaid with Sharpies, just last night.

her actual socks

She walks MILES!

Ms.Wu wears KEDS so she can cover the school.

Here are the feet of the principal, Ms. Wu, taking my feet to my new homeroom. Bye, Momo.

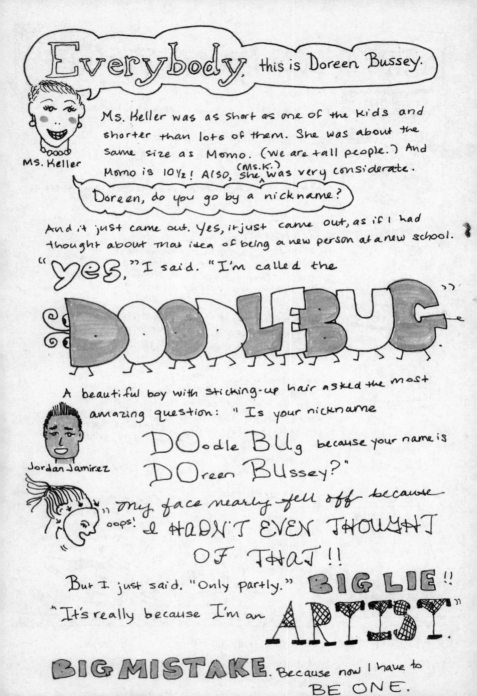

Everybody, this is Doreen Bussey.

Ms. Keller

Ms. Keller was as short as one of the kids and shorter than lots of them. She was about the same size as Momo. (We are tall people.) And Momo is 10½! Also, (Ms. K.) she was very considerate.

Doreen, do you go by a nickname?

And it just came out. Yes, it just came out, as if I had thought about that idea of being a new person at a new school.

"YES," I said. "I'm called the

DOODLEBUG."

A beautiful boy with sticking-up hair asked the most amazing question: "Is your nickname

Jordan Jamirez

DOodle BUg because your name is DOreen BUssey?"

"Oh! My face nearly fell off because I HADN'T EVEN THOUGHT OF THAT!!

But I just said. "Only partly." BIG LIE!!

"It's really because I'm an ARTIST."

BIG MISTAKE. Because now I have to BE ONE.

BUSSEY, DOREEN D. 7K KELLER

	1	2	3	4	5	6	7
M	SPAN 112	SCI 345	SOC ST 218	PE	LANG ART 313	ART 016	MATH 201
T				SHOP / LUNCH		CHORUS 011	
W				HOME ARTS / LUNCH		STUDY	
T				SHOP / LUNCH		CHORUS 011	
F				PE / LUNCH		ART 016	

"**O.K., 7K,**" said Ms. Keller, picking up this schedule thingy of mine, "**Who's got SPANISH** in 112 with the **Doodlebug?**"

An Indian girl (Asian Indian) with **LONG BLACK BRAIDS** came over to me.

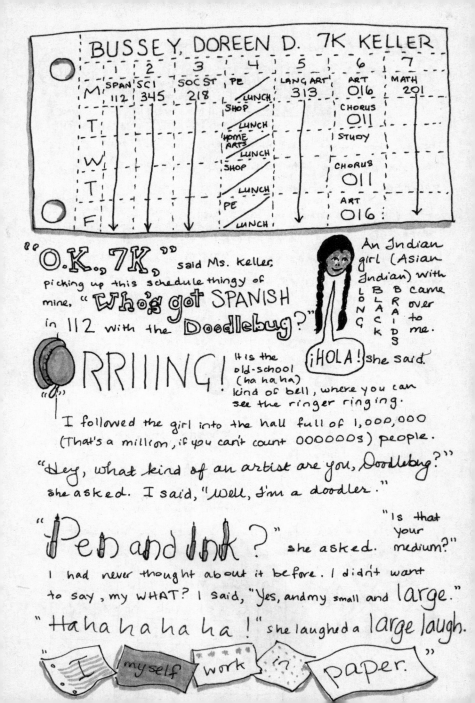

ORRIIING! It is the old-school (ha ha ha) kind of bell, where you can see the ringer ringing.

"¡HOLA!" she said.

I followed the girl into the hall full of 1,000,000 (That's a million, if you can't count 0000000s) people.

"Hey, what kind of an artist are you, Doodlebug?" she asked. I said, "Well, I'm a doodler."

"**Pen and Ink?**" she asked. "Is that your medium?"

I had never thought about it before. I didn't want to say, my WHAT? I said, "Yes, and my small and large."

"Ha ha ha ha ha!" she laughed a large laugh.

"I myself work in paper."

Español was only two doors down the hall.

The teacher wasn't even there yet so we sat down and the girl pulled a little folded-up paper out of her backpack. She turned a corner of it up and asked, "Can you draw something RED, just in this triangle?" "What RED?" I said. "ANYTHING!" "Cherries?" "Yeah!" I could tell there was some SPEED involved here.

Quickly, I drew cherries, then an orange, a lemon,

beans, a blueberry, a bottle of ink, a sheet of paper,

and a pig. Just the head.". There wasn't time for "¡ *Muchas grácias* !"

my new *amiga* said.

She stood the folded-up paper on her desk. *Turns out, it was her homework.*

7Q	Pinho, Marco	✓	✓-	✓
7K	Kaur, Elizabeth	✓	✓	✓+
7E	Soldano, Sarah	✓+	✓+	✓+
7B	Furniss, Richard	✓	✓	✓
7K	Bussey, Doreen	—	—	—

The assignment (over Christmas vacation, of course) was to come up with a creative way to test people on Spanish vocabulary.

"What IS that thing?"  I asked.

Instead of answering, she just showed me:

She said, "pick a day of the week." I picked Sunday. "That's domingo," she said.

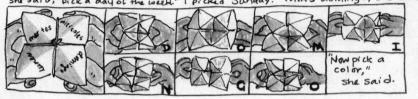

"Now pick a color," she said.

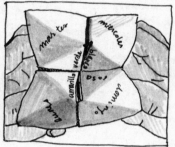

I picked amarillo.
She folded the thing out flat:

"Name something that's amarillo," she said.

I said,  "¡BUENO!" she said.

And she opened the corner of the thing where it said amarillo.

THERE IT WAS: my LEMON!

"What IS this thing?" I said.

"It's a Cootie Catcher," she answered.

The class was going on so I wrote Elizabeth Kaur a note:

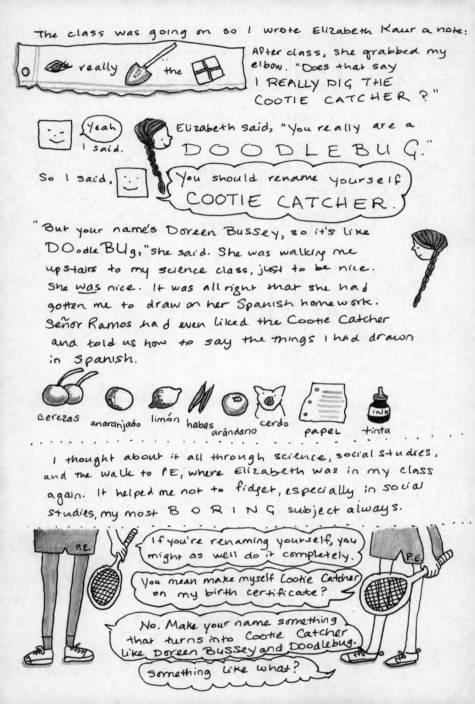

really the [eye] [shovel] [window grid]

After class, she grabbed my elbow. "Does that say I REALLY DIG THE COOTIE CATCHER?"

Yeah I said.

Elizabeth said, "You really are a DOODLEBUG."

So I said, You should rename yourself COOTIE CATCHER.

"But your name's Doreen Bussey, so it's like DOodle BUg," she said. She was walking me upstairs to my science class, just to be nice. She _was_ nice. It was all right that she had gotten me to draw on her Spanish homework. Señor Ramos had even liked the Cootie Catcher and told us how to say the things I had drawn in Spanish.

cerezas   anaranjado   limón   habas   arándano   cerdo   papel   tinta

I thought about it all through science, social studies, and the walk to PE, where Elizabeth was in my class again. It helped me not to fidget, especially in social studies, my most B O R I N G subject always.

If you're renaming yourself, you might as well do it completely.

You mean make myself Cootie Catcher on my birth certificate?

No. Make your name something that turns into Cootie Catcher like Doreen Bussey and Doodlebug.

Something like what?

"*Colleen* Callahan"

??? I know it sounds a little Irish or something, but..."

Irish! But she's

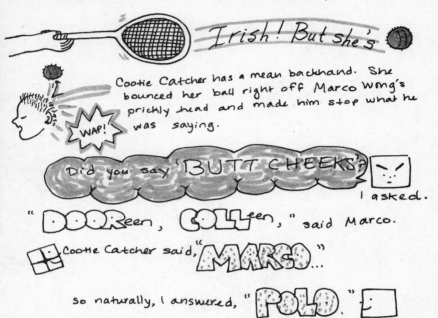

Cootie Catcher has a mean backhand. She bounced her ball right off Marco Wong's prickly head and made him stop what he was saying.

WAP!

Did you say 'BUTT CHEEKS'? I asked.

"DOOReen, COLLeen," said Marco.

Cootie Catcher said, "MARCO"...

so naturally, I answered, "POLO."

Marco went, ...grumble grumble grumble grumble...

"whassamatta, boy?" I said. "You got rocks in your mouth?"

HE said, "AT HOME, I HAVE 64 *prismacolor* PENS."

(I bet he had at least 8 greens in that bunch, the color(s) I could have turned with pure JEALOUSY.)

Cootie Catcher said, "We all know they're your dad's, Marco."

AND MARCO said:

4. Monday DRAGS ON

"You should call me MAGIC MARCO."

Cootie Catcher SNORTED. "Just because your dad's an illustrator, you don't have to think you're such an ARTIST."

"Just because you know ORIGAMI doesn't mean you're such an artist either, ELIZABETH."

I felt like I had the POWER.

o o o (Peace to all people) I thought. Out loud, I said,

My mother says everyone is an artist.

Cootie Catcher said, "I HAVE MY DOUBTS ABOUT THAT."

She could be a little mean. Were they enemies? I needed help in this school. I made a decision.

I just didn't say anything else.

If they wondered what I thought (not just my mother), I was giving no more info.

I was like the Sphinx, this big statue that is half lion, half man, in Egypt. People ask it questions, but it doesn't answer, so they have to figure it out themselves.

O WELL.

There are not this many pyramids there, but I just like them!

I was also like Sven, keeping his thoughts to himself under the bed. In Staci's apartment, was Mom trying to find a job?

In art class, there was that triangle face again.

NO. NOT MO- MO.

STOOLS RULE

1. You sit up higher.
2. You sit up straighter.
3. You can turn around without scraping the floor.
4. You can wrap your feet around the legs.

AND ART HAS STOOLS!!

Plus, you can stand up to work anyway,

I never get in trouble, in ART.

"How come you don't have your PRISMACOLORS?" I asked. "Where are your pens, Magic Marco?"

"My dad's worried something will happen to them at school." Magic Marco looked a little suspicious. "What about you?"

I SHOWED HIM THE TOOLS OF MY TRADE:
Pilot P-700 fine point

Faber-Castell Pitt artist pen brush-point in light grey

"I WORK IN BLACK + WHITE."

I didn't want him to think I cared too much about all those Prismacolors. I didn't have a single one to my name, but Dad used to have the use of them at his old work, so their wondrousness is known to me. But I don't have one, so I can't draw one here — and anyway, here came the art teacher,

MR. HILL, who looked like black ALBERT EINSTEIN.

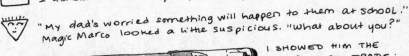
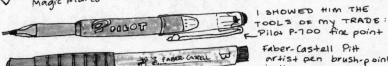

BOMBS AWAY!

Doodlebug? Well, let's see what you can do with CLAY

WOOSH!

WHACK!

SPLAT!

He threw clay and yelled!!!

The Stages of CLAY

DO WE HAVE TO YELL WHEN WE'RE WEDGING CLAY?

They put me down in the basement because I am a troll and nobody cares if we make noise here.

First, it is underwater in a river or lake, so it has water in it. It needs to stay wet.

FAIR ENOUGH!

I became a wedging champion at that moment.

BOOM!

Whack!

So you dig out a lump and dry it with rags.

Use a wire to cut some off.

"There will be air bubbles inside."

Mr. Hill says loudly, "while you're wedging, think about what you'd like to make with your clay." wedge wedge wedge wedge wedge wedge wedge wedge wedge

I'm going to make a model Sven. It can keep him company under the bed or remind Staci what he looks like on days when he won't come out.

Now WEDGE it! Throw it down HARD! over and over!

IN CHINATOWN, there are statues of waving cats. I think I'll make a "beckoning cat" to wave to Sven. Maybe he'll realize the world can be an okay place.

If you don't wedge clay enough, then what you make will have air in it, and it will blow up or crack in the kiln. SO WEDGE IT!!

WWAM!

That afternoon,

I told him about it as I lay next to him under the bed. It was what happened the last period that had sent me there. COULD BE BAD.

It took **4** Band-Aids to patch me up.

:("Thanks, Mo," I said sadly.

△ "What did you DO to him, anyway?"

(ME do to HIM*??)

* Sven, of course. Evil Sven.

"All I did was TOUCH him."

dumbcatrottencatmeancatstupidcatdidn'the knowl wanted to love him??

△ Momo wouldn't let it go. She never lets things go. She said again,

"What happened?"

:("He was scared," I said. "I wanted to make him feel better. So, I tried petting him. I guess some cats don't like petting."

Poor baby! We looked up and Mom was in the doorway. She had on her job interview clothes, which she had bought in L.A. when we decided to move here. Paper doll Mom.

mousse-y, organized hair...

"Tell me all about your day," said Mom in a way we knew meant not to ask about hers.

light gray suit with nautical flair...

buttoned-up shirt (red+white)...

"Sven ATTACKED DODO," said △.

control-top panty hose...

:("I was just trying to pet him."

...and worst of all, real shoes, at least they're red.

"It's going to take PATIENCE, Dodo."
→ → → → → → → →

"**Everything** takes **PATIENCE** !!!"

☹ I 😠 yelled 👿 impatiently. ☹ "And I don't HAVE any!!"

MOMO was using up all the BAND-AIDS sticking them on herself.

She said, "□□ O DO, I think you had patience right up to the moment you tried touching Sven."

☹ I said, "If you don't try, how will you ever know?"

"😖" Mom shook her head, thinking to herself, and said, "Exactly right." Then she added, "Tell me more."

(TELL ME MORE. That's what she always says when we come home from school to tell her stuff. But it feels like a million years since I heard her say it -- way back in December, before I got expelled but after the Ritalin started but before I started just <u>pretending</u> to take it, after I found it made me feel like the tortoise in the story of The Tortoise and the Hare. <u>SLOW AND STEADY</u> is NOT how I want to run the race.)

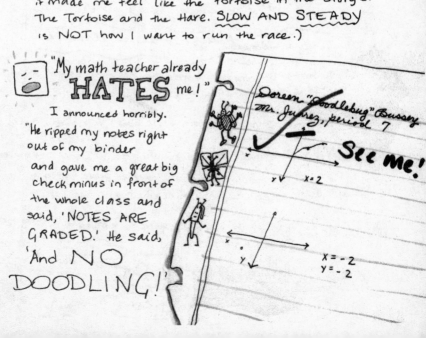

😩 "My math teacher already **HATES** me!"

I announced horribly.
"He ripped my notes right out of my binder and gave me a great big check minus in front of the whole class and said, 'NOTES ARE GRADED!' He said, 'And NO DOODLING!'"

Doreen "Doodlebug" Bussey
Mr. Juarez, period 7

✓

See Me!

$x = 2$

$x = -2$
$y = -2$

"THEN, YOU CAN'T DOODLE."

I will die if I cannot doodle. It's just that simple. Mr. Juarez is going to wreck my whole plan of survival at this cool school where I already have two nice friends and where I know new words in Spanish and where you can play tennis and wedge clay with a crazy Albert Einstein genius teacher (well, I mean I don't play tennis with Mr. Hill but it might be jolly).

Your plan of survival at your new school is to doodle?

"OBVIOUSLY!" I said.

momo said, "But you'll get in trouble." "OBVIOUSLY!" I said again.

But WHY? "Because I found out =

Things are better when I draw."

It sounded like one of Mom's sayings that sound good, but I wasn't exactly sure what it meant.

Maybe, or maybe not, Mom knew how I felt. She said,

Number 1: I believe it. I'd go cuckoo if I couldn't write.

Number 2: But you are going to have to prove it to your school by doing really really well.

Number 3: Or you are going to have to consider trying the Ritalin again.

momo said, **Number 4:** Doodle Power!!!

But leave Sven in peace. "I will," I said.

Then Mom said, "**How was your day, Momo?**"

I felt very small, then. Because I hadn't even asked.

"*Fine,*" said Momo. Well, that's what she always says. But...

I said, "But?"   It was her eyes. She was worrying.

"What?" Momo asked me. I shrugged my shoulders.
I waited. I knew what I knew.
Then she said, "There's a choir at our new school.
You have to try out. I never tried out for anything
before. And I really want to get in it. There aren't even
any spaces because it's the middle of the year. I probably
won't be able to do it and then you can't try again until
September and maybe we won't even be here then, you
know, because it might not work out for everybody else.
But they do a giant concert in that ~~beautiful~~
CATHEDRAL and they perform at the Moscone Center and—"

"**I get it!**" I said. Somebody had to stop Momo before
she fell completely to pieces over how I
might screw up school for her!

"*Momo, baby,*" said Mom. "The **wonderful** thing is
that you like it here. This situation is a ~~great~~
~~opportunity~~ ~~for~~ all of us. We all want to make
the most of it — Dad, you, me, Dodo — "

"**and Sven!**" I said. "He is expanding his horizons, too."

"*Yes,*" said Mom. "We all are going to just keep on
doing our ~~best~~ to be our ~~best~~ selves. And Dodo — "

"**Sing something,**" I commanded Momo. "Sing
'River Deep and Mountain High.'" This is an old
Tina Turner song that Momo learned off Dad's iTunes.

And the way she sings, we're all sure: She's IN.

SOME MORE THOUGHTS ON MR. DUFFY

He said that learning to keep your thoughts and questions to yourself was part of maturity and that people with self-control kept their hands still and

Dodo, hon, I don't want to set your sister up for failure. How competitive do you think things ARE in that new school?

I haven't really thought about it. There are a lot of kids, but that means there's lots to do. But, competitive...?

I think I'm going to call and ask them to let her try out for that choir.

She's sure good enough. Listen to her!

She's never had to try out for anything before. This is all new.

Everything's different now for everybody.

It's all good.

But what if Mr. Juarez is like Mr. Duffy?

It's just one class out of seven. Mr. Duffy was ALL DAY.

That's for sure. And I didn't have

DOODLING.

Mom said, "Let's leave Sven to hold the fort" and took us on a bus ride all the way here, to the Palace of Fine Arts. I think that it is the

Most gorgeous place in the city

'and maybe the World!!

There is the crazy fog that comes here, and the top of the bridge and Momo the Martian Singing Girl is standing on the cliff singing out to it all.

"MOM!" I yelled. "What time is it?" She showed me:

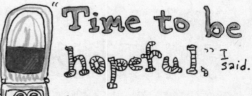

"Time to be hopeful," I said.

"Oh, Doodlebug Dodo, that's what I love about you," said Mom.

Momo + me hanging off the bed upside down.

On the bus ride home, we were all three **very quiet.**

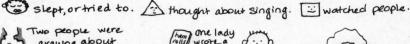
slept, or tried to. thought about singing. watched people.

Two people were arguing about whether HE had flirted with some other woman.

A lady in a newsboy hat read a book about somebody called Captain Jack. It sounded dirty.

One old man just stared out the window and waited for his stop.

One lady wrote a list for the grocery store.

ham rolls mop vmm ulah blah blah blah

monkey man hung on the bar and chinned himself

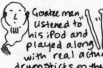
Goatee man listened to his iPod and played along with real actual drumsticks on the window. Nobody told him to stop!

As usual some girl had a video game blocking her face from the real world.

As usual there were some battling cell phone people.

If Mr. Juarez had these people in his class, they would almost all * get in _trouble_!

Back "home," Dad was waiting with sweet & sour chicken and Sven was eating a rib under the bed.

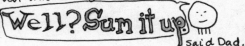
Well? Sum it up
said Dad.

So far I could write for an underwear catalog or labels for cough medicine.

I don't think being able to sit still is that important.

Ribs...tasty!

I never had to try out before.

My new boss is into old Elvis Costello and he has a dartboard with HIS boss's face on it.
So much for MONDAY!

5. MR. JUAREZ

and Other Dangers

SECRET:

Even though Mr. Juarez wrote "See me" I didn't go see him. It was last period so I went and met Momo and we went home.... In the middle of the night I sleepwalked. That's what must have happened because suddenly I banged into something, and I realized I was in the kitchen at the sink in the pitch dark at 3:13 a.m., and guess what? Sven was there with me.

I GUESS I HAVE TO GO SEE HIM, SVENNY.

I believe it's best, Dodo.

I'm not telling about sleepwalking. They are all worried enough.

I think Sven has forgiven me for scaring him under the bed.

 **IN THE MORNING,**

in homeroom, I wrote this note. Cootie Catcher showed me how to fold it into an envelope. On the way to Spanish, we dropped it at the office.

Dear Mr. Juarez,
I do not doodle to be disrespectful. Doodling helps me to pay better attention. I would like to have a chance to make up the √–. And I would like to ask permission to doodle on a separate piece of paper so it won't be on my notes.
Doreen Bussey

:("What do you think he'll say?" I worried to C.C.

"It's a reasonable request," she said.

I waited on 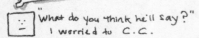 PINS and NEEDLES until finally it was 7th period, when MR. J. **Just Said NO.**

"**NO**, grade makeup?" "**NO**, non-note doodling?" "**NO**," said MR. JUAREZ.

"**NO**, special rules for one student that don't apply to others."

"But this is **DIFFERENT**," I said. Just then I saw:

It was Momo, too upset to wait for me outside the door.

KNOCK! KNOCK!

AT FIRST, Mr. Juarez was really sweet. He opened the door and asked kindly,

"*who are you?*"

"**Momo!**" I said. "What happened?"

"They said **NO**!" she bawled.

"The CHOIR people? How could they?" I asked.

"I was so nervous, I could hardly sing!"

I BLEW IT!

Maybe Mr. Juarez meant to be nice. He patted Momo's shoulder, saying,

"*That's such a shame. Well, try again next year.*"

Maybe I should have let it alone. But instead I spoke up.

"**NO**, that's WRONG!" I said. "You should hear Momo sing!"

Mr. J said, "But the CHOIR people heard her sing."

"**NO**, she was nervous!" I said. "She never had to try out for ANYTHING before. They knew her voice in our old school and she always just got PICKED."

Mr. J said, "Was that school right about EVERYTHING?"

Momo dried her tears extremely quickly. "**NO**,"

she said. "They were all wrong about **Dodo**."

"It's **DOODLEBUG** now," said Mr. J. "Isn't it?"

"But not in **MATH**," I said. Mr. J. said, "Doreen,

"...I took a look at your file today."

(drumroll) "Is it okay to talk in front of your sister?"

"Momo knows all about me," I said.

Mr. Juarez said, "So... borderline A.D.D.* And a somewhat optional medication that you opted out of."

I decide to open up my box of secrets a tiny inch. "I would rather handle things my own way than take stuff."

MR. JUAREZ is young for a teacher. His face is mostly nose, mustache, and eyebrows.

Permanent Records: PUNKS ☠

Bussey, D.

* Attention Deficit Disorder

FOR THE FIRST TIME, his eyes smiled. (I know that sounds weird, but.)

I'm impressed by that.

"YOU ARE?" I was somewhat, borderline surprised.

"Then why can't I..."

"BREAK MY RULES AND DOODLE?"

he asked.

"Yeah," I said. "Why?"

His eyes went all serious again. "What makes you think you need to doodle?"

I flipped my lid then. "To stop from doing all that A.D.D. stuff!!!!!!"

(momo held her breath.) (But Mr. Juarez did not ASK.)

He said, "There's more than one way to skin a cat."

GOOD THING SVEN WASN'T HERE TO HEAR THAT!!

"I mean," said Mr. J., "if you can do it one way, you can do it another way. Find some other ways."

Momo announced, "I am going to be in CHOIR."

Cootie Catcher was waiting in the hall.

"This is Cootie Catcher," I said. "This is Momo."

"It's really Elizabeth," she said. And Momo said,

"Miss Maureen Bussey. I'm going to sing 'O Beautiful' over the P.A. tomorrow."

"Get out, you are NOT!" said C.C.

"WAIT FOR IT!" said Miss Maureen Bussey. "And there's not going to be any choir teacher watching!"

HEAVEN HELP US °° I thought.

Momo was mad at herself, so watch out !!!

"So, did Mr. Juarez say you could doodle?" She looked like she already knew. SLY.

"No. And he meant it."

"YUP," she said cheerfully. "When Marco had him he crunched up a whole art paper Marco was working on in math."

THAT'S Wrong!

"Have you two ever been HOMESCHOOLED?" asked Cootie Catcher.

"No. Why?" Because you think you own the world!

HA HA HA HA HA HA HA Momo and I laughed. "Why shouldn't we?" I said.

But Momo said, "We don't even own a CAT."

When we got home,

Dad was working late.　Momo was singing "O Beautiful."

I was drawing CC's beautiful braids.　And Mom said, "STOP EVERYTHING! I have to write about underwear."

HORRORS!
TIGHTY WHITIES

WHAT? KIND? OF? UNDERWEAR? AND WHY?

"It's a tryout," said Mom.

They're from the company, they're not Dad's.

what's this hole for? Eww!

Mom has to make you want to buy them.

"oh, no!" said Momo, then stopped herself.

"Tell me what's nice about them," said Mom. Ha Ha

"They're nice and **white**," said Momo. Ha Ha Ha

"They're SPICY and *TIGHT!*" I said. Ha Ha Ha Ha

"Okay, get out of here and let me work!" said Mom.

"But first, tell me how you like your underwear to feel."

We like it when she asks us this serious sort of work question.

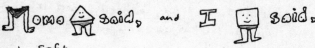

Momo said, and I said.

1. soft
2. silky
3. short (not hanging out all over the place)
4. not pinchy

1. clean
2. cool
3. comfy (no wedgies hahaha)
4. pretty

How was your day, Svenny?

I love you, Sven.

Then we got under the bed and talked to Sven.

He didn't have anything to say in return.

Momo said, "What's it like to be so scared?"

"Momo," I said, "how come you think you can sing on the P.A. if you were too scared in the choir room?"

"**EASY**," she said. "Nobody will be looking at me."

We left Sven alone under the bed after that.

We made meatballs and SPAGHETTI.

Dad came home and said, "All I did today was draw diagrams of eyeballs!"

eeka freeka!

The meatballs are the monster's eyeballs!

I wish I could just DRAW all day.

The spaghetti is his brains.

where's your mother?

underwear!!

From the bedroom we heard Dad say, "what kind of a manager is on the phone ALL DAY?"

At dinner, everybody sure was tired......
After, we piled on the couch and watched TV.

WHATEVER!

purrrrr

Underwear: it's fun-to-wear! No...

Listen to Sven!

Well, tomorrow's another big old day....

zzzzzz

I have to keep reminding myself that today is only Tuesday. It isn't even one week since we left L.A. I like it here, the cable cars, the fog, Cootie Catcher (mostly), Mr. Hill and the clay, and Sven, who isn't even ours. I don't want us to get thrown out again, even if Mom has to write underwear catalogs, Dad has to draw eyeballs, I can't draw, and Momo can't sing. But I'm going to draw. And Momo says she's going to sing. I didn't tell Mom or Dad what she told me and C.C. Tomorrow's going to be a big old day, all right.

What a Wednesday!

SCHOOL OFFICE

First of all, Momo made us late. When we finally got to school, HOMEROOM had started.

Hang on a second, Dodo.

In that **second**, Momo stopped by the office. The MORNING ANNOUNCEMENTS hadn't started. I leaned close to the door and heard my sister say,

"Hi, I'm Maureen Bussey? And I was asked to sing 'O Beautiful'? At the start of announcements? Is it time now?"

And the secretary must have turned on the P.A.

O beautiful for spacious skies, for amber waves of grain...

Our little Momo sang that whole long song and she sounded like a ROCK STAR and when she was done, she said,

This has been MAUREEN BUSSEY in a song dedicated to Mr. Juarez for his inspiration.

And the school secretary said, "Thank you, Maureen. That was *Lovely.*"

This is the COW I almost had.

HAVE YOU LOST YOUR MIND? WHY DID YOU HAVE TO DRAG MR. JUAREZ INTO IT? NOW I'M GOING TO BE IN TROUBLE AS WELL AS YOU, AND I WAS ALREADY IN TROUBLE WITH MR. JUAREZ!!

Ms. Keller said, "Doodlebug? Was that your sister?"

YES I felt proud.

"She's got the music BUG," said Cootie Catcher.

In homeroom,

Señor Rámos asked, "Dorena, la cantadora, ¿es tu hermana?"

"Is the singing girl your sister?"

"SÍ," I said.

In Spanish,

We talked about waves — water waves, sound waves, and music waves. I could draw.

In Science,

I listened to this whole big long thing about the civil war. I already had it in my old school. I doodled. And doodled. Until a hand came down on my book and Ms. Farley said, "I FIND THE DOODLING VERY DISTRACTING."

In Social Studies,

We talked about home safety.
1. KEEP YOUR DOORS LOCKED.
2. LEAVE A NIGHT-LIGHT ON SO YOU DON'T KILL YOURSELF FALLING OVER SOMETHING IN THE DARK.
3. CHANGE BATTERIES IN SMOKE ALARMS.

In Home Arts,

Magic Marco asked, "Can I sit with you?" "Was that your sister on the announcements?" "What do you like best, chisel point? fine point? brush point?"

All I can get!

ART NERD!

At Lunch,

We are reading the worst book in the world, Lord of the Flies, and we had to talk about

"Do rules matter?"

"Some rules hurt people," I said. Then I shut up. Why ask for trouble?

In Language Arts,

By the time I got to study hall I was half crazy.

I took the lav pass and ran out, straight to Mr. Hill's room.

"Can I wedge clay? PLEASE!"

HAM

And then there was Math.

Mr. Juarez watched me like a HAWK. I didn't dare to DOODLE.

and at the end he said, "DOREEN? ME."

1. I ran upstairs to language arts to pick up my extra assignment, because I wouldn't participate in the class discussion.

2. Detention with Ms. Farley for too much doodling.

3. Marco: Hey, Doodlebug, I have something for you! (It's a folded-up paper.)
   Me: Have you seen my sister?
   Marco: Sorry...

4. I went to see if Momo was by any weird chance in the chorus room (nope: empty) on my way to helping Mr. Hill put away the clay I wedged.

5. Then it was back up to see what Mr. Juarez wants NOW!

"I know, I know," I said. "I should have stayed when you asked. But I'm already **in trouble** with you, so what does it matter? I had to take care of things with all my other teachers. Well, not **ALL**. Just some. But the other ones will probably check in tomorrow. **Anyways**, I have to go now and find my **sister**."

Mr. Juarez just looked at me funny.

As politely as I could, I said, "Mr. Juarez? <u>What?</u>"

He said, "You haven't seen your sister?"
Then he added, "Why did she say I inspired her?"
I looked at him. He really DIDN'T KNOW!

"You made her mad!" I said.

He said NOTHING. While I waited,
I opened the paper Marco
had given me.

"WHAT'S THAT gorgeous thing?"

It's a...

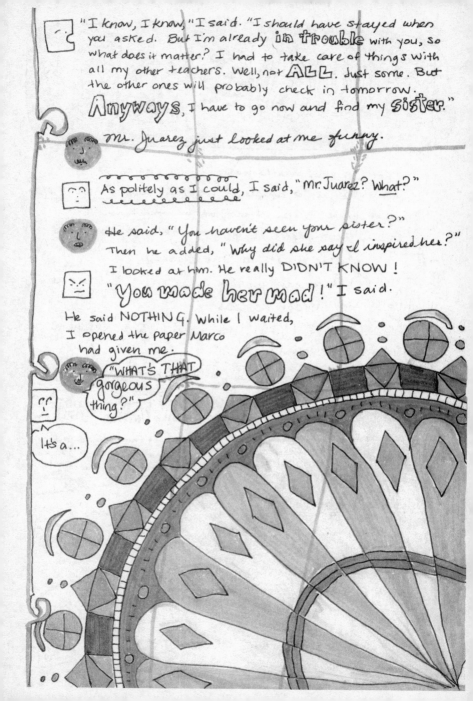

DOODLE!

"It's very mathematical," Mr. Juarez said.

"It's just a doodle," I said. "But Magic Marco must have taken it out of the trash in Ms. Farley's room after I got in trouble for making it."

"In her class?" Mr. Juarez asked.

"Yes," I said, glaring. "And Marco 'colored' it with his Prismacolors."

"Marco Pinho?" Mr. Juarez said. "Is he a friend of yours?"

I blushed. "Can I please go home now?"

"Sure," he said. "WAIT. TAKE THIS."

He scribbled quickly on a sheet of paper and addressed it to my parents.

m/m Bussey

"m/m means mr. + mrs.?" was all I could say.

I left him the doodle. I read the note as I walked down the hall.

m/m Bussey —

I would like to talk to you. Please give me a call at your convenience.

JJ
555-1700 x259

RATS!!

"I'll expect an answer tomorrow,"

said Mr. Juarez.

As I went home, I felt like a ~PSYCHO.

Q. Where was Momo? Why hadn't she waited for me?

Q. What did Mr. Juarez want to talk to m/m Bussey about? How were they going to get time to go to school to talk? It was obvious that I was just plain in trouble anyway.... And maybe Momo was, too.

PITCH IN!

A. The Letter got HEAVIER as I walked, then ran, then walked. I DIDN'T KNOW if I wanted to HURRY HOME or never get home. AT LAST I did what Cootie Catcher would have done, and

I changed the shape of the PAPER (from a letter to TRASH)

Meanwhile, at home... Mom was writing STICKIES:

Don't talk to me, I have to think about UNDERWEAR.

speaking of Psychos...

protective casing for the family jewels

cotton-y linen-y tight-y white-y

PANTS without RANTS- just RAVES!

marshmallows clouds sheets teeth vanilla ice cream black paper ivory light polar bear

Sticky Underwear?

Stays white all night

Won't fray all day

smooth cool refreshing

makes you feel like a kid again!

Won't ride up no matter what horseback riding bicycle riding tango dancing

you won't even know they're THERE!

WHERE'S MOMO?

HERE'S MY SUGGESTION: "MOON OVER S.F.!"

6. I DON'T KNOW WHAT TO CALL THIS CHAPTER.

Sven, Swedish kitty, you should have been there when **Momo** sang. She rocked the **school**, Sven, and you'd have been **proud**.

Momo didn't talk to me for a long time, so I talked to Sven and listened to Mom typing. Finally, she said, "WHY DON'T YOU LEAVE SVEN ALONE?"

"BECAUSE, I like him."

"WELL, he doesn't like you!" She sat up. She had been crying....

"Mo, how come you didn't wait for me?"

"I was in DETENTION!" (WHOA! That never happened before!)

? "HOW COME?" (But I had my suspicions.)

"Ms. Wu! The PRINCIPAL! For lying to the secretary about the P.A. I hate this school!"

"I DON'T! I don't know why, but I don't!" (This was only half a lie.)

Then Mom came flying in!

"**DODO**! Is this your idea of HUMOR? Do you think it's funny to make fun of my WORK? Do you think it's easy to sit here all day coming up with something that's going to make people buy ugly old boring tighty whities as if they were something NEW and EXCITING?"

NO, Ma. Sorry, Ma.

But: After she went out, Momo LAUGHED. "Ma, I thought it was funny!" SILENCE.

uh-oh.

"You know what I think was **funny**? You dedicating your song to MR. JUAREZ! And fooling the secretary! And then singing it all perfectly like you did! ALL DAY LONG, people asked if you were my SISTER! And I said, 'Yeah, she ought to be in choir!' And they said, 'SHE SURE SHOULD!'"...

...*I knew I was right but something made me stop talking. Maybe it was the look on Sven's sphinxy face, but I didn't say to Momo, 'I'm sure they'll let you in the choir.' Because I sure wasn't sure. Not at all.*

Well, what else was there to do? We did our homework...

Doreen Bussey
Ms. Michaels per. 5

Do Rules Matter?

In class I said some rules hurt people and I really think that's true. Okay, there are good rules like change the batteries in your smoke alarm or don't steal from people. But what about rules that give you only one chance to do something you're really good at, like my sister and singing, or rules that say you can't do something that will help you learn because teachers think if they let one kid draw then everyone will and then the whole school will be

There I was, cranking away, when suddenly Momo went insane.

"I CAN'T DO IT!"
"I DON'T GET IT!"
"THIS SCHOOL IS AHEAD OF US AND I DON'T UNDERSTAND!"

Homework Exercises
I. Convert to decimals.

1. $3/4 = .75$

2. $5/8 = $ _____

3. $16/17 = $ _____

4. $1/25 = $ _____

5. $3/10 = $

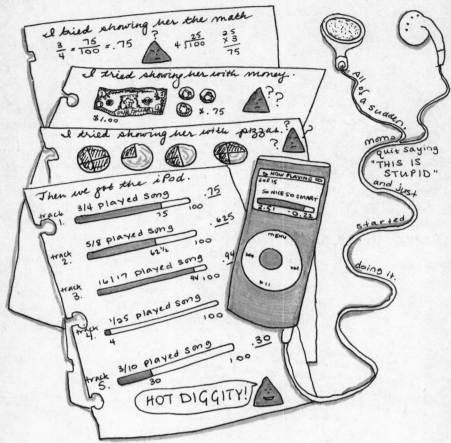

I tried showing her the math

$\frac{3}{4} = \frac{75}{100} = .75$?

$4\overline{)100}$

$\begin{array}{r} 25 \\ \times\ 3 \\ \hline 75 \end{array}$

I tried showing her with money.

$1.00 $.75   ??

I tried showing her with pizzas. ?

Then we got the iPod.

NOW PLAYING
2:06:15
SO NICE SO SMART
2:51   -0.22
MENU

track 1.   3/4 played song   .75   75   100

track 2.   5/8 played song   .625   62½   100

track 3.   16/17 played song   .94   94 100

track 4.   1/25 played song   100   4

track 5.   3/10 played song   100   .30   30

HOT DIGGITY!

All of a sudden, momo quit saying "THIS IS STUPID" and just started doing it.

Dad came in. That's how late it was!
"Sometimes you just need a VISUAL," he said.

For once I felt proud. QUICK, before he could ask us, I asked, "How was your day, Pops?"

His face changed so FAST. "Unbelievable."

Then he said, "MY BOSS got the  AXE.

It was his own fault. He got caught talking to his girlfriend while throwing darts at the president of the company."

Mom was in the doorway. "Not the REAL president?"

"No, the picture on the dartboard!"

"Who caught him doing it?"

"Who ELSE?"

HA HA HA HA HA HA

"THE PRESIDENT!"

Dad got very serious. "It won't be funny if I lose

my job."

Mom got serious, too. "I'd better get down to business with this underwear ad. Could everybody please get out of here?"

ORT! ORT! ORT! ORT!
ORT!
ORT! ORT!
ORT!
zzz

Dad took Momo and me to the wharf where

SEA LIONS

were barking at the whole entire city, and after that, well, really, there was no place we wanted to live so much as the beautiful and amazingly great

San Francisco!!!!!

It was very late when we got home, and Mom was asleep, and the folder of her work was sitting on the kitchen table looking done. The LAST THING I was going to do was tell anyone about Mr. Juarez and his NOTE.

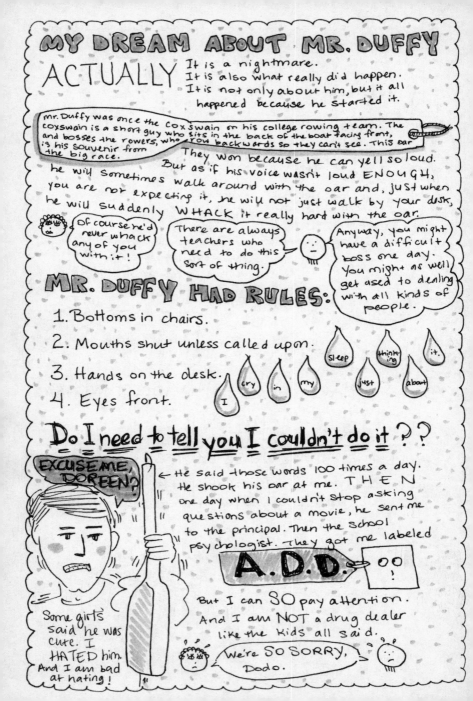

7. MOMO FINALLY GETS LOST !

I sat on the stairs of Staci's apartment and called for Sven until Dad woke up. He said, "You can't make a cat do anything —"

"Why?" I said. "Do they have attention problems?"

"They're just independent thinkers," said Dad. He rigged up the door so it stayed almost shut but Sven could still get in if he came back.

"IF?"

By morning, there was still no Sven.

"MOM will be here most of the day."

"most?"

Dad was grumbling: "I'VE got to go to work to see IF I'VE STILL GOT A JOB."

Mom was mumbling: "You'll be a sight tonight in your TIGHTY WHITE BRIEFS."

blue →
blue →
blue →

Momo was fumbling in her closet, digging through looking for blue clothes. "Dodo, do you have anything ROYAL BLUE? NO, that's not! Yes, that is!"

SVEN!!

I was STUMBLING around exhausted, calling to Sven.

When we left, he still wasn't home.

← yellow

SAN FRANCISCO

blue blue blue blue

"**Cootie Catcher**, where's everybody going?"
"Not EVERYBODY, just the choir," she said.
That explained the blue choir robes. Hmm.

"It's the first Thursday of the month. We sing
at the MOSCONE CENTER."
Hmm. Hmm. "Full bus," I said. It was
CHAOS the way field trips are, but
the choir robes made everyone look neat. They
just had them on top of their regular clothes.
Hmm.   Hmm.   Hmmmmmmmm.

I walked away S L O W L Y.
"Who's that, Elizabeth?" said the girl next to her in line.
"You don't know the **DOODLEBUG**?" said ▦. "You WILL."
The bell rang for Home.room. 🍎🍎 went
running by in a streak of BLUE. "Don't be late again!"
"I ALREADY CHECKED IN!" Momo called.

If I had a red marker like Mr. Juarez, I would
use it to color in Magic Marco's face and ears,
but you will have to imagine how he
looked when he saw me that morning.
(hint: He was red.) + brown eyes, like ooood.

How'd you like your doodle?

"It's beautiful," I said.
I WAS blushing a little too. My face was so hot.

"Nobody ever put color in anything I drew," I said.

It was a long, nerve-wracking day.

HOMEROOM

where was Sven?

"What are the school colors?" I asked Marco.

"Royal blue and grey, like the BAY and the FOG."

"Mr. Juarez called our doodle gorgeous," I told Marco.

ESPAÑOL

Sven, come home.

SCIENCE

Without the choir kids there, we just did book work in Spanish. I went out with the lav pass two times to deal with the jitters in my legs. I learned a new sentence. I didn't see Momo anywhere, but it's a big school.

Science! My kind of class!

We were playing with SLINKYS.

Svenny! Svenny!

This was supposed to show how SOUND TRAVELS but I disagreed.

This isn't WORKING for me!

"EXCUSE ME, DOREEN?" asked Mr. Travis.

I said as quietly as possible:

"I think this is how one little ping might travel through the air, like the slinky moves, but not another sound."

Maybe if he had asked me to elaborate I would have clammed up like yesterday in L.A. when we were discussing Lord of the Flies.

BUT he gave me a box of STUFF. "SHOW ME."

And there was a jump rope in there. I laid it on the floor and pumped one end up and down and kept doing it.

"VERY INTERESTING IDEA!" said Mr. Travis.

At the end of class he said, "GOOD THINKING!"

In Social Studies the LAV PASS was my friend again. I can't just sit at a desk and read. Even though I was more tired than usual, I was also more nervous than usual. How could I NOT be, with Sven missing? How could I NOT be, with Dad working at a job he might lose any minute? How could I NOT be, with Mom needing so bad to get the underwear account? How?

and then there is Mr. Juarez waiting for my parents to call and waiting for me AT THE END OF THE DAY?

was Mom looking for Sven?

→"Oh no, you don't, Miss Ants-in-the-Pants!"

"But, Miss Farley!"

"No buts!" she said, and turned away.

I got up and went to the window and looked out.

I saw MY FATHER walking into the school.

"Miss Farley! Can I go —"

"Doreen, take your seat."

I got out my pen and pad. I would quietly write her a note, explaining.

"I'LL TAKE THE WRITING IMPLEMENTS," said Ms. Farley.

((NO!))
NO WAY! NO! NO! NO!
NO DICE! NO HOW!
NOT NOW NOT EVER NOT IN THIS LIFETIME!
I YELLED.

"Excuse me, Doreen?"

Every eye in the room was looking at me.

I've been trying to tell you, but you haven't been listening. My father is here! I need to tell him something about my sister.

You don't need your sketchbook for that. You're far too interested in what's going on in IT and in other parts of the school. NOW, just take your seat, Doreen.

"You don't understand!" I said.

Well, PERHAPS you would like to explain AFTER SCHOOL....

I don't think anyone uses the word PERHAPS who isn't being SARCASTIC.

"No," I said. "My sister is missing and my cat is missing, so I have to go right home today. I won't have time to come see you, so can I please have my sketchbook back NOW?"

"I don't think so," Ms. Farley answered.

I didn't think. I just left the room.

Trouble Time

Dad?

218 down the hall

downstairs

to the office

MS. WU pushed a new button on her phone. VERY CALMLY, VERY QUIETLY, she asked the person on the other end,

Would you please take a look on your bus for Maureen Bussey?

Sixth grader.
Brown hair.
No choir robe.
I'll hold the line.

"Don't worry," I said to Dad. "That's where she is."

WHY?

She wants to sing in the choir, that's all.

MS. WU said into the phone, "YOU'VE GOT HER?"

Dad made a giant SIGH. He talked into his phone.

Jolene? They found her. Guess where? She sneaked onto a school trip with the choir.... Dodo guessed it. Yup.

MS. WU asked me, "How did you guess, Doreen?"

I said, "I think she was dressed in

camouflage

She had on royal blue, like San Francisco Bay."

"WHY?" asked Dad.

"So she could Sing, that's all," I said.

But MS. WU asked, "Why are you angry?"

I said, "MY SISTER is a GOOD SINGER."

From the outer office, the secretary called,

"She's the one who hijacked the P.A. to sing 'O Beautiful'!"

"She did WHAT?" said Dad.

I said, "She deserved a SECOND CHANCE."

The secretary called, "Elspeth said she fell short when she agreed to give her a tryout."

I said, "She never TRIED OUT at our old school."

"And it wasn't HER fault she had to leave, it was MINE."

MS. WU asked Dad, "Are you surprised by any of this?"

"Actually, I am proud of all this."

And that is when Ms. Wu told me I could go back to class. But not to Ms. Farley's, that was over. I made it for the end of Shop, too late to work on anything. There are STOOLS in shop class, same as art, and I sat on one with my feet on the other, and stared at my toes.

magic Marco

is in my class. He was painting his birdhouse in colors fit for a parrot.

"THAT'S SO PRETTY," I whispered.

He handed me a gold prismacolor.

"You look like you need some color in your life," HE SAID.

At lunch, the choir was back.

DODO! DID YOU HEAR?

 "Did I hear what? That you ran away with the choir in CAMOUFLAGE?"

 "So that's what the royal blue outfit is all about?"

 "You can sing, Maureen. Did they suspend you?"

 "There's a meeting tomorrow with Ms. Wu and the choir teachers and me and Mom and Dad. But that's not what I wanted to tell you—"

 "You think they might <u>suspend</u> you?" (To myself I said, "Or expel you?" Oh, no!!)

 "Mom called!" said Momo.

 "I'll bet she did!" said Cootie Catcher.

 "Dodo, LISTEN," said Momo. "Mom said the lady upstairs called on Staci's house phone. They know

where Sven is!"

 "WHERE !?!?" "Up the TREE!" "Oh, NO!"

But Elizabeth Kaur/Colleen Callahan/Cootie Catcher said,

"HE'LL COME DOWN SOONER OR LATER.
MY FATHER IS A FIREFIGHTER AND HE SAYS
THERE'S A REASON WHY YOU NEVER SEE

any CAT SKELETONS up in the TREES!

well. Thanks
Colleen!

In Language Arts, Ms. Michaels made me read my opinion essay to the class. When I was finished, she said,

LANGUAGE ARTS

"DOREEN, AND EVERYONE ELSE, what do you think you should do if you decide a RULE is Wrong?"

SVEN IN THE TREE

I didn't say anything. Other people said:

O Riot!
O Rewrite the rule.
O Break the rule.
O Talk to the person who made the rule.
O Just leave.
O Quit and tell the boss why.

clipper-onner

She wrote them on the board with a chalk pen ← pusher-upper

chalk   chalk pen body

Imagine the writing is white!

Ms. Michaels said, "DOREEN? You have a voice."
I said, "If you don't try to change things, then
NOTHING will ever change." Duhhhhhhhh

Chorus Time

AND THEN, IT WAS CHORUS TIME.
It's just a class for singing. I don't think it's anything like CHOIR. Everybody in this school has to take chorus. I certainly don't have any "TALENT."

Hang in there, Sven.

As I stood there singing, I thought about the rule-breaking. MOMO had broken rules just trying to get what she wanted. But wasn't what she WANTED the right thing?

AT THE END of the class I went up to Mrs. King. I noticed SOOTIE SATCHER behind me trying to listen. I didn't care!

Mrs. King, what if you tried out for choir and you didn't get in? What if OTHER STUDENTS knew you were a good singer and they got up a PETITION to get you in the choir? How many signatures would you need?

What if every signature was on an origami BIRD and we hung them all over school?

Mrs. King gave us a very fishy eye look.

You're Maureen Bussey's sister, aren't you?

YES, AND SHE SINGS LIKE TINA TURNER!

Run along, girls.

I've got a thousand paper cranes! I made them after I read this book but I had nothing to use them for! Everybody who wants Momo in the choir could sign one!

AT LAST (you guessed it)

Juarez Time

It was period 7. Math time. Juarez time. My sketchbook was in Ms. Farley's desk. He wouldn't have let me Doodle anyway. He was going to ask me why my parents hadn't called. He was going to keep me after and write me another note and

I'm coming, Sven!

- - - - - - - You guessed it. I cut class. - - - - - - -

I did not dare go home early. I sat next to the mailbox on the corner and waited for Momo. Then we walked home together.

"Oh boy, whatta day," said Momo.

"All I want to think about is Sven," I said.

Oh, thank goodness !!!!

1. Mom did not say a word about school.
2. She just scooped her work folder off the table and headed for the door.
3. "I have to go down and present my revision," she said.
4. "I've been watching Sven since Mrs. Broccoli called this morning. I had just come from my FIRST MEETING. She said he was on the grass until he saw her dog, Henry. Then up he went, up the tree."
5. She pointed toward the living room window, the one right over our bed.

Oh, Sven! How did you get OUT THERE?

8. MOMO AND I ARE

Ring
Ringy
g Ring
Ring

4A

"Good Cat, Sven!"

When we finally got Sven home, the phone was ringing and the message light was going cuckoo.

Momo answered. "Hello?"

Then she said, "I'm sorry, he's not here."

And then, "No, sorry, she's not here either."

And then she said, "Um, okay, just one second."

She gave me the phone and whispered,

"MR. JUAREZ!"

Carefully, I put Sven down on the floor. He made a dash for his safe place under the bed. Back to that!

Hello?

Doreen, this is Mr. Juarez, your math teacher.   ← like I forgot!
I haven't heard from your parents about that note I sent home yesterday   ← we know why that is!
and I missed you in math class today   ← I didn't miss you!
but I note that your parents have a meeting at school tomorrow at nine
regarding your sister   ← oh, really?
and so I thought I'd ask them to join me and a few other faculty   ← my other teachers?
at ten o'clock in Ms. Wu's office.
Have them call if there's a problem.
Any questions, Doreen?   ← a PROBLEM?? Yeah, there's a PROBLEM! A BIG ONE!

"NO QUESTIONS!" I said.

I hung up the phone...

I said, "MO? They're meeting about you at nine?"

She only nodded. "They never met about ME before."

I said, "CONGRATULATIONS!"

She said, "They're meeting about you, too?"   (fireworks)

I said, "MOMO? We're DOOMED."

 "...me?"

momo and I just looked at each other.

 Oh, boy. We're in TROUBLE now.

mom and Dad looked at each other, then at us.

"Well," I said. "*The good news is Sven is back.*"

Then Mom asked Dad, "What meeting do YOU have?"

"The big CHEESES at work," Dad said.

"They're meeting to discuss my proposal: I told them I wanted to take over the department."

Dad said to Mom, "I thought your meeting was today."

"It WAS," she said. "And they basically REJECTED everything I'd worked on. And then they picked up an idea that was just a STICKY on the inside of my folder. It was that underwear MOON thing of Dodo's."

"OH, NO!" I said. "Oh, Mom, I'm so SORRY!"

"Dodo, they *laughed*!" Mom said. "And they gave me three hours to work it up. They're meeting about my revision TOMORROW."

MOMO said,

"SO neither of you has to be AT the meetings?"

"NO," they said.

"Good," said me and Momo.

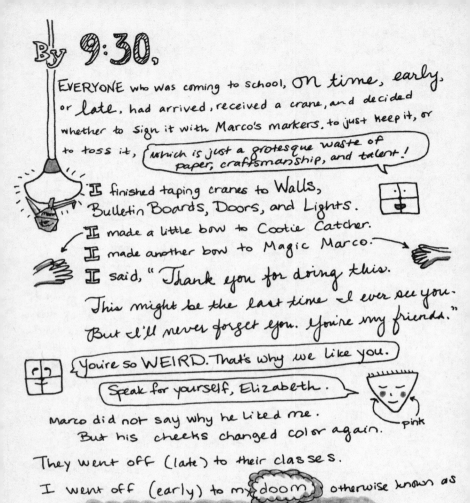

By 9:30,

EVERYONE who was coming to school, on time, early, or late, had arrived, received a crane, and decided whether to sign it with Marco's markers, to just keep it, or to toss it, *which is just a grotesque waste of paper, craftsmanship, and talent!*

II finished taping cranes to Walls, Bulletin Boards, Doors, and Lights.

II made a little bow to Cootie Catcher.

II made another bow to Magic Marco.

II said, "Thank you for doing this. This might be the last time I ever see you. But I'll never forget you. You're my friends."

You're so WEIRD. That's why we like you.

Speak for yourself, Elizabeth.

— pink

Marco did not say why he liked me. But his cheeks changed color again.

They went off (late) to their classes.

I went off (early) to my doom, otherwise known as

MS. WU'S OFFICE

"You're not until **10**, lovey, so just take a seat," said that same secretary. (Inside the office, I could hear voices: Momo, Mom and Dad, Ms. Wu, and that same choir teacher.)

I said, "I don't even know your name yet." The secretary said, "I'm Mr. Stein."

Mr. Stein said, "Ms. Wu, I'm so sorry!

Ms. Wu sighed. "The Bussey girls!"

I stole a glance at my sister. "Wait'll you see, Mo."

"See what?" they all said.

"They are cranes for choir," I said.

"But I'm not IN choir," said Momo, who didn't get it.

"YOU ARE NOW," said Ms. Wu, who did.

MOMO'S PEACH FACE LIT UP. "THANK YOU!" she cried.

"Don't thank ME," said Ms. Wu. "The people have spoken."

"AND YET," Ms. Wu added, "what kind of a precedent do we set if we reward illegally stowing away on trips?"

"Are you going to suspend me? Expel me?"

Ms. Wu sat down so she could look Momo in the eye. "Would I let you in choir and expel you from school?"

for two seconds, I felt better. Then Ms. Wu asked me,
"Doreen, who's responsible for the choir cranes?"

I was silent.
But then I said, "**NO**, I won't tell you."

And Ms. Wu said, "That's what I thought you'd say."

And she _smiled_.

"**Girls**," she said. "I'm going to stay here for a few minutes and talk to your parents."

INSIDE MY STOMACH
Butterflies began flying.

Momo and I thought we'd just wait outside but

Ms. Wu said,
"Mr. Stein?
Please send the Bussey girls to bring down Elizabeth Kaur and Marco Pinho."

oh no, oh no, oh no. Ms. Wu didn't need ME to name the culprits!

What's going on?
My meeting's over! Why am I still here?
Wow, thanks for the cranes!
You're an alto, right?
I wasn't even supposed to bring all the markers. My Dad...
SLOWER... SLOWER... SLOWER...

Meanwhile, back at the office, it was ten o'clock and Mr. Juarez had showed up. I could hear his voice — and (oh, no!) Ms. Farley's. Mrs. King must have stayed. That other deep voice was Mr. Hill's... and the woman laughing? Ms. Michaels!

"**NEVER!**" she sang out. Then it got quiet again.

We waited.

We didn't wish to discuss things in front of Mr. Stein.
I don't know what Momo the Peach P.A. hijacker was thinking.
I don't know what Elizabeth/Colleen/Cootie Catcher was thinking.

I don't know what Magic Marco was thinking, either.

I thought of o o o

Sven

Mr. Duffy

My Sketch-book

the Sea Lions

Marco's pink cheeks

"Doreen, come in, please," said Ms. Wu.
Everyone – parents, teachers, principal – looked at me.

"Thanks, Doreen. Would you tell us, please,
what you think of our school?"

MS. WU called on MS. FARLEY.

Doreen seems to have a problem with rules. She needs to understand that a school makes rules for the good of all the students, and that they can't be changed because, for example, some one wants to DOODLE in class.

My Dad said, "Dodo, it's time for you to explain why you decided to become

The Doodlebug

when you came to this school." Mom nodded.

I said,

"I found out it helped me keep stiller.
    I could think clearer when I was doodling.
    I didn't need to get up and go out all the time.
    I could listen and pay attention."

Ms. Farley said, "She <u>does</u> go to the lav too much."

I said, "Because you yelled at me for doodling and then took away my notebook!"

Ms. Keller said, "I think we know more about alternative learning styles than we are acting on."

you mean old cow!

I kept my thoughts about Ms. Farley to myself.

Mr. Hill said, "I think Doreen's pretty fair at figuring out what she needs to do."

Ms. Michaels said, "Doreen could be a SHINING STAR at this school if we gave her a voice."

Ms. King said, "She certainly has made some STEADFAST friends in her first four days."

And then MR. JUAREZ spoke up.

He said," 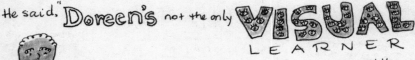 **Doreen's** not the only **VISUAL LEARNER** in this school. She's not even the only one with an ALTERNATIVE LEARNING STYLE. But she— and her friends outside— seem **uniquely** able to figure out how to bring out the best in themselves and others. Here's a

SHOW & TELL :

what is...

what is this thing? cootie catcher

"Señor Ramos suggested I take a look at Doreen's 'how to' for paper-folding."

"There are directions for wedging clay, too," said Mr. Hill.

("Vital skills!" muttered Ms. Farley.)

" There's a very scientific diagram of the eyeball," said MS. Wu. "Mr. Travis wrote me a note about that — and a few other demonstrations Doreen did in science."

(my eyeballs were popping at the idea of everyone checking out my sketchbook. But it seemed to be backfiring on MS. FARLEY, who must have offered it up.)

MS. Keller contributed, "That's a very nice picture of the school."

MS. King pointed out the music for "O Beautiful."

"Now for math,"
said MR. JUAREZ.

MIDDLE SCHOOL

"She draws patterns," he said. →

"Good grief," said Mom.
"Hoo boy," said Dad.
(They were smiling.)

"She made a Venn diagram ← of her parents' opinions on Jr. high."

"She draws mathematical doodles, like an Altair design — and she got a friend to provide color!"
(I blushed.) →

track
1. 3/4 played song
.75
75 100

track
2. 5/8 played song
.625
62½ 100

"And whoever heard of using an iPod to teach decimals?"

"I thought of it myself," I said.

Exactly!" said Mr. J.

M
S.
W
U
Said

"I'd like Doreen — el mean, The Doodlebug — to work on the section of the school Web-site that's dedicated to homework support. And if she can prove that her doodles are helping her learn other subjects besides math, maybe we can find ways of sharing the doodles with other kids."

"SHE'LL HAVE A TOUGH JOB CONVINCING ME," said Ms. Farley.

Let me try!
I said.

9. THE END

Then Ms. Wu opened the door and let Momo, C.C., and M.M. in. The teachers all filed out. Mr. Juarez squeezed my shoulder as he went by.

Then Mom and Dad got up to go. Their eyes were full of words they didn't need to say to Momo and me, because it was like we could hear them.

"**Good Luck!**" said Momo, and then I snapped to attention and said it, too.

Ms. Wu looked questions at us. "It's a big day for all of us," said Dad.

"They have MORE meetings," said Momo.

"WHEW!" said Ms. Wu. "Some days are like that. Just one second..." and she sat down in front of Cootie Catcher and Magic Marco in that way she had with Momo. She made them a speech:

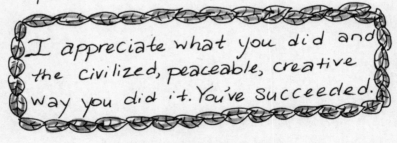

I appreciate what you did and the civilized, peaceable, creative way you did it. You've succeeded.

And right away, Momo started singing
"O Beautiful!"

COME TO CHINATOWN.

That is all Mom and Dad said to me and Momo when they
came home that night. Momo and I had been wondering and
worrying all day, and so, I think, had Sven. Just when
he was getting used to us, wouldn't it just be terrible
if everything for them went wrong, just when school
was looking better for Momo and me?

They
wouldn't
answer
our
questions!!!
"FIRST
THINGS
FIRST,"
they kept
saying all
the way to
C-town....

Finally, we got
to this store
Mom wanted
us to look in.

"See those
STAR
lanterns?
I want both
my ☆s to
choose one."

I picked a purple one. Momo's was gold. "Where are we
going to put them?" Momo asked.
"In the front window over your bed?" said Mom.
"But, Mom," I said. "Did you get the thing? Are we staying?"
Dad said, "Get a waving cat, too."

fish kites

fortune
cookies

tangerines

It was going to be Chinese New Year soon
and there were lots of good luck objects.

When we had our star lights, Dad said, "WELL.
Both of our answers were very nice *maybes*.
I am interim manager. Interim means 'for now.'"
And Mom said, "I'm making a sample underwear ad."

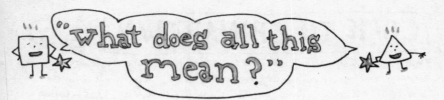

"what does all this mean?"

It means, we're staying in S. F. for now.

It means, Sven is our own cat for now.

It means, Dad's job is safe for now AND
he gets a tryout for another one.
(And yes, Momo, he IS nervous, but hopeful.)

It means, Mom gets to try out with my idea
for the Tighty Whitey ad, plus her words:
Reliable cool serene familiar bright

It means, for now it's a pretty happy ending.
(and that's the luckiest
you can be sometimes)
and maybe, just maybe,
definitely maybe
we'll be able to stay
here for good, here
where we like our school
and our school (mostly!)
likes us, here with the
sea lions in San
Francisco, under
the underwear
moon.

The End   D.B.

P. S.

Naturally at school it is not all starlight and fortune cookies.

These girls came up to me in gym class and they said,

DOODLEBUG! Do you think you're so great just because you can **DRAW?**

I said,

Would it be greater if I couldn't draw?

But it made me feel very small...

But I felt a little **bigger** when Mr. Hill told me that by **middle school** most kids lose art confidence. (~~I am so glad this didn't happen to~~ me .)

Mr. Juarez— How about some artistic support for the web page?

http://www.it'sdifferentfromathleticsupport.hahaha/

So, you think you're **NOT SO GREAT** because you can't draw? I have **2 WORDS** for you:

Ed Emberley

Ed Emberley's BIG ORANGE DRAWING BOOK ★★★

and I hope nobody minds if I write him a little advertisement because anyway it's my new career besides he rocks because he will make you feel like you can draw cool things like alligators and tanks **PLUS** he understands how you might only have enough money for one **marker.**

He shows you how to draw things so you won't think it's all so **impossible** and maybe you will feel how I do if I sing in the shower, like maybe there's

"hope"

so just don't listen to anybody who says,

Is somebody doing something to the CAT or is that you singing?

click here for help drawing cats!

O **THINK** drawing is in your **BRAIN** not your **Hand**,

So either PLAN your picture out of shapes like Ed E., or like Momo says this girl Lily in her class makes cats:

Meow!

cartoony (PLAN)

or LOOK really hard at a cat and try to copy the way I did drawing Sven 800 times:

realistic (LOOK)

If you want to know how bad my drawing from looking can be, look at my tower mistakes at the beginning in Ojai!!! Oh, the horror! But even then I was hooked! I was the Doodlebug even though I stunk because I didn't care!

Here is a partial list of things I love to draw:

seagulls

alphabets + shadows

ladybugs

cupcakes

fancy drinks ("Shirley Temple," no alcohol)

baseballs (Go, S.F. Giants!)

Volkswagen Beetle

chicken triangle

crazy guy

my name in lights!

pencil

dead-tired doodlebug

Try it! IGNORE MISTAKES. Doodle on, **DUDE!**

Go Fish!

GO FISH

KAREN ROMANO YOUNG

What did you want to be when you grew up?
An author and illustrator. Really. From about age six, when I realized people created books.

When did you realize you wanted to be a writer?
I was always writing and drawing, no matter what else I thought I was doing—taking classes or working in other fields, such as science, teaching, nursing, library work. . . .

What's your most embarrassing childhood memory?
I'd better not share this with your impressionable audience!

What's your favorite childhood memory?
Trips with my grandmother to the World's Fair and the Empire State Building . . . going to Ocean City in the summer with my family . . . building things like basement booby traps and backyard cities with my friend Neil . . . taking art classes . . . the Mets winning the 1969 World Series.

As a young person, who did you look up to most?
My parents, who were always making things and showing me how to make things . . . Karen Whitney and Arne
Bass, the children's and young adult librarians at my
wonderful library, the Fairfield Children's Library . . .
Linda Perry, my art teacher . . . Joy Shaw, who ran a local
ecological organization focused on the river that runs
through our neighborhood.

What was your favorite thing about school?
Jump rope. I went to a parochial school with no play-
ground, so we jumped rope: regular jump rope, double
Dutch, and Chinese jump rope.

What was your least favorite thing about school?
Gym class. Crazy nuns. Getting in trouble for doodling.

**What were your hobbies as a kid? What are your
hobbies now?**
Exploring woods, wetlands, and beaches, often with a dog
or a friend. Painting, drawing, collaging, sewing, making
things, building things. Reading. Swimming. Still doing exactly the same things.

**What was your first job, and what was your "worst"
job?**
First job: babysitting. I volunteered at the children's library
when I was thirteen and continued to work there for pay
once I was old enough, all the way into college. Worst
jobs were boring summer things I did, like bookkeeping

and filing for a company that sold propane gas. I literally counted the minutes. . . .

What book is on your nightstand now?
Caddy's World by Hilary McKay; *The Fault in Our Stars* by John Green; *The Tiger's Wife* by Téa Obreht; *Feynman* by Jim Ottaviani.

How did you celebrate publishing your first book?
I was in Ocean City when I got the news, and went out and told my whole family on the beach. First, I asked them why they thought I was smiling. . . .

Where do you write your books?
In my barn, in my car, in the Reading Room of the New York Public Library's big library on Fifth Ave and 42nd Street.

What sparked your imagination for *Doodlebug*?
I always liked telling stories with speech bubbles and little drawings, and decided to try a full-length story—a book!

What challenges do you face in the writing process, and how do you overcome them?
The biggest challenge is freaking out in the middle because I'm afraid that the work is not as good as I hoped it would be, or that the story is not how I envisioned it, or that basically, it stinks. A couple years ago, I heard *Horn Book* editor-in-chief Roger Sutton ask Brian Selznick how

winning the Caldecott Medal for *The Invention of Hugo Cabret* had changed his work. Brian said that he now realized that the place of terror he had inhabited while working on *Hugo* was the place he needed to be in order to go forward. The terror meant that he was pushing ahead out of his comfort zone and challenging himself to create new things. I repeat this to myself continually.

Are you a Doodlebug?
Yes.

Have you ever moved to a new city?
Not as the family does in *Doodlebug*, no, but I did go away to college and away to work at a summer camp and away to London for a semester, so I know what it is like to go somewhere where nobody knows you, aware that you're going to have to stay for a time, and considering how to re-create yourself with a new group of people.

Which of your characters is most like you?
The very most me is the heroine of a not-yet-published book called *Hundred Percent*, but there is also a great deal of me in *Doodlebug*, in Cherie in *Outside In*, and in Daisy in *The Beetle and Me*.

What makes you laugh out loud?
Dogs.

What do you do on a rainy day?
Paint.

What's your idea of fun?
Snorkeling.

What's your favorite song?
This is a very hard category for me because I like almost every kind of music. "No Sleep Till Brooklyn" by the Beastie Boys. "Bewitched, Bothered and Bewildered" by anybody. I love the new music Arcade Fire did for *The Hunger Games*, and lots of opera, including Puccini, Mozart, Orff, Gilbert & Sullivan, and others. I could go on and on about this question, but you get the idea.

Who is your favorite fictional character?
Mortimer the raven in Joan Aiken's books.

What was your favorite book when you were a kid?
The Saturdays by Elizabeth Enright.

Do you have a favorite book now?
Winter's Tale by Mark Helprin.

What's your favorite TV show or movie?
My So-Called Life.

If you were stranded on a desert island, who would you want for company?
My husband. Or Mortimer.

If you could travel anywhere in the world, where would you go and what would you do?
Antarctica, to work with scientists studying everything from microbes to orca.

If you could travel in time, where would you go and what would you do?
What comes to mind are superhuman things like stopping the slave ships in Africa, stopping the trend toward climate change, stopping the Nazis. I'd also like to travel with explorers.

What's the best advice you have ever received about writing?
When I sold my first novel, my friend, the writer/editor Deborah Kovacs said, "Now write another one." This idea—that the focus of work has to be forward—has driven my writing life, and saved me from obsessing about what happens to a book when you finish it, which is that it goes out of your hands and out of your control.

What advice do you wish someone had given you when you were younger?
Write what you would want to read (not "what you know").

Do you ever get writer's block? What do you do to get back on track?
No. I've never experienced this. I do get off track, however, because of worrying about whether something is going to work out well. E.L. Doctorow famously said that writing is like driving home at night: You can only see as

far ahead as the headlights, but you can get all the way home that way. The message is to keep working, no matter how slowly.

What do you want readers to remember about your books?
That it is all right to be yourself, whoever you are.

What would you do if you ever stopped writing?
Drop dead. I can't stop writing.

What should people know about you?
I actually LIKE my hair the way it is.

What do you like best about yourself?
I really do enjoy MYSELF.

Do you have any strange or funny habits? Did you when you were a kid?
I used to quietly, politely break rules to see what would happen. I used to just walk out of class or school to see what would happen, expecting people to chase after me. I walked through storage areas in stores, or the freezer at the grocery store. I walked in the out door of big public events. Nobody ever questioned me. I learned that if you act like you know what you are doing, people will not question you. Pretending you know what you're doing helps you get away with a lot.

What do you consider to be your greatest accomplishment?
My three wonderful, grown children.

What do you wish you could do better?
Write and draw. I work at it all the time. I have a long way to go.

What would your readers be most surprised to learn about you?
I am not afraid to fly in any kind of plane or helicopter (or spaceship, if I had the chance) or to scuba dive or dive in a submarine, and I am not afraid of sharks or spiders, but I can't go to scary movies or anything with the word "horror" in it.

SQUARE FISH

Doreen's determined to make her new life in San Francisco work. But it's not easy, considering her ADHD, her younger sister's popularity, and financial stress at home.

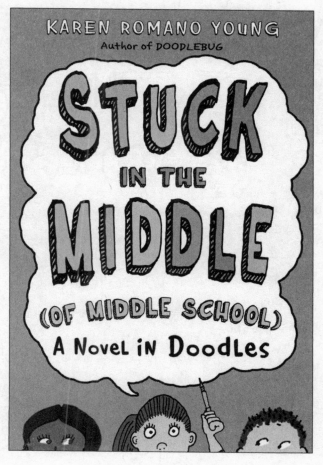

Turn the page for
STUCK IN THE MIDDLE
(OF MIDDLE SCHOOL).

1. Tighty Whitey

THINGS are good. are great!

Elizabeth Kaur / Colleen Callahan or, as she is known in these parts, the **COOTIE CATCHER**, is telling Momo's fortune with her paper-folding arts.

"You will become a world-famous opera singer, Maureen."

"NAH, I'm going to be a **ROCK STAR.**"

And Mom says, "That's Momo for ya. She never settles."

In the kitchen, Magic Marco Pinho says, "You mean, nothing's ever good enough for her?"

(HIS CHEEKS ARE EVEN PINKER ⋅L⋅ THAN WHEN HE GOT HERE, AND THAT WAS ALREADY PRETTY PINK!)

"Not a bit!" says Dad. "She doesn't let what anyone else says or does **LIMIT** her."

And then he makes a great *proclamation:*

"**EVERYBODY SHOULD MAKE THEIR OWN STOP SIGNS IN LIFE.**"

"Hooray for that idea but isn't it time to get *going?*"

This is the reason we are all here together at our house. All together, we are going to witness **MOM'S** big cottony moment:

We drove out of the city and came back until suddenly we saw it !!
I bopped Momo on the head and said, "THAT'S MY MAMA!"
She waved both hands and yelled, "THAT'S MY MAMA!"
Dad sighed," IT'S GORGEOUS, JO!"
C.C. said, "Those are the biggest undies I've
ever seen, Mrs. Bussey. Impressive!"
Marco said, "Your very own sign."
Mom said, "You are all very sweet." And smiled.

We dropped M.M. and C.C. off on our way home.

Marco
Magic Marco

lives in a tall, modern apartment house on top of the HIGHEST hill.

"SWANKY!" says Mom.

Elizabeth
Cootie Catcher

lives in the cutest cottage in a long row of cute cottages. "Cute, but crowded." she says.

"If only I was an ONLY child."

But she has 4 sisters.

Bye! Thanks!

Bye Marco!

Bye! See you tomorrow!

Bye Cootie!

"That's a SWEET house," says Dad.

"What does his father do?" asks Dad.

"He's a graphic artist," says Elizabeth.

"Oh, so it CAN be done!" says Mom.

"It doesn't take a lot of money to be happy," says Mom.

There was a silent space in the car. "Well, that's good!" said Momo. "Since we don't have a lot of MONEY."

Dad didn't answer.

I said, "Yeah, well, pretty soon, TIGHTY WHITEYS will be on all the big shots in the city!!"

MOMO said, "You mean all the Big Butts!!"

Mom said, "From your 👄 to God's 👂 👂."

I asked, "What will you buy?"

Mom said, "A SWEET little house."

DAD said, "No, a SWANKY apartment."

Momo asked, "Can we take SVEN?"

And we all answered, "Sven is Staci's cat."

Momo said, "Maybe he is just a little bit ours.

If EVERYTHING around here feels like
it is just a little bit ours, that is
because we have tried to make it so.
By now it is ALMOST our house, our apartment,
our stairs, our neighborhood, our roof, our cat,
our city, our school, our life. But guess what?

Staci comes home in just 3 days.

We are maybe moving into a little house near
the Cootie Catcher's cute cottage. It is for rent.

Yes, sir! We are staying.

DAD is still interim manager for now.

MOM's underwear is all over the city. Hee hee.

♪♫ MOMO has a solo in the choir's
~~spring~~ concert.

AND ME?

I am the UNSTOPPABLE, AMAZING,
TROUBLESHOOTING, BRILLIANT,
THRILLING, CHILLING, KILLING......
(turn the page!)

And Sven comes out and
listens to us when we talk,
but still won't let us pet him.

(you guessed it, art fans!)

Doodlebug

That's me!

(Also known as Doreen Dolores Bussey, Dodo for short)

AT HOME AGAIN, we were all very quiet. Strange!!

Mom sat in the kitchen looking out the window.
(She looked a little like the tighty whitey moon: serene. Full.)

Momo and Dad were sharing the iPod.
"What are you listening to?" I asked.

They said, "WHAT?"

I laughed, and they looked befuddled.

↑ 50¢ WORD

FIFTY CENTS

Dad was nibbling on the headphone wire like he always does, so I took it out of his mouth, like Mom always does, but she wasn't seeing anything right now. So I wrote her a note instead of talking.

Dear Mom, I always knew you could do it. I'm so proud of you.

THE " 📱 " RANG AND I ATTACKED IT!

It turned out to be for me, anyway: Elizabeth.

Doodlebug? Did you see the WEB SITE?? It's so great!!

I went to get Dad's laptop.

Of course, Cootie Catcher was talking about my

Fabulous Page,

which has, so far:

* iPod division
* coloradoodle
* graph how-to
* study helps

▶ Venn diagram
▶ cootie catcher
▶ sound waves

"THANKS, COOTIE!"

I said. "There's lots more to come. There's gonna be a timer, a schedule, a decision-maker (sort of magic 8 ball), plus spelling disasters and a podcast and movies and ..."

"AND AND AND STOP!!"

said Cootie Catcher.

It's on the school web site: FAME!

There it was again, the Stop Sign in Life.)

 WHAT?

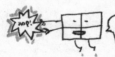 The great big BURST on the bottom! where it says April Fool Hop!

"What's the April Food Hop?" I asked. I swear, there is always some crazy new thing to deal with at this school!

"FOOL, fool!" said C.C. "It's a dance, young lady."

"Will there be food?" I asked. "In our old school in L.A. they had discos and the best part was the marshmallow fights."

"Here, the best part is the BOYS," said Cootie. Then she asked,

"Are you going to go with MAGIC MARCO?"

I tried to act bored. I almost yawned.

Sure. I'll go with you, too, Cootie. Okay with you?

Well, yo, I mean this is San Francisco and all, and we can carpool, fine, but my actual date is going to be... my cousin WALDO from Palo Alto.

WALDO?!

Yeah, and if you want to know where he is, just shut up. If you want to know who he is, he's my parents' friends' son, he's not my real cousin, and they thought it was a cool name, that's why he's called Waldo, and why am I going with him? Because he's adorable and he's 14 and I'm passionate about him.

So why do you call him your cousin? →

Parents are so deluded. →

Maybe they could call him Wally for a nickname. →

14! He must have a beard. →

The only person I'm pass— ...ut is Sven. →

And he's a CAT.

I said, "SO?"

She said, "SO, you and Marco could go as a COUPLE and we could DOUBLE and I wouldn't get in TROUBLE because I'm not allowed to date yet."

oh man, oh man

Marco + me = couple of what?

double date? Oh, I'm in trouble, bubble.

Mom? Am I allowed to date yet?

WHAT?   WHAT?   "   "   WHAT?

Cootie, I've gotta go.....

Yeah, they heard THAT all right.

We didn't look at each other, we looked out the window. It was easier that way. Mom **tried** not to pry, and I tried not to have a **tantrum**. It wasn't what you'd call an easy conversation and we could only **hope** Dad and Momo were iPodding again.

"MOMO, YOU'D BETTER NOT BE LISTENING."

We talked softly so she couldn't. Mom said, "You could ask Marco, you know, Dodo."

I said, "What the heck is the point of a **double date**?"

"Makes it easier sometimes," said Mom. "You're not stuck with just one person trying to talk."

"Do I **HAVE** to?" I asked. "Just because the Cootie Catcher wants to?"

"Does it have to be a big deal?" said Mom. "I mean, you'd probably go with the two of them anyway. They're your **best friends**. Just like you brought them tonight."

"That was **COOL**," I said. "I'd rather just have it be Cootie. WHY does she have to bring this Waldo guy?"

WALDO!! said Momo. "GET OUT OF HERE!" I yelled. GRRRRRRR.

trudge   trudge